Padma Shri Pran

Maurice Horn, the editor of World Encyclopedia of Comics, has described cartoonist PRAN as Walt Disney of India.

Entertaining generation after generation, his comics have been constant companion of all the growing youngsters providing fun and amusement through his famous characters like CHACHA CHAUDHARY, SABU, SHRIMATIJI, PINKI, BILLOO, RAMAN etc. More than 600 of his titles are selling well in the market, and numerous comic strips are regularly appearing in various newspapers. His CHACHA CHAUDHARY comics had already been adapted for a TV Serial, and ran continuously for 600 episodes on a premier channel.

Travelling widely over the globe, he delivers lectures at various International Conferences. He has also been honoured with 'People of The Year Award' by Limca Book of Records for popularizing comics. His comic book 'United We Stand' was released in 1983 by the then Prime Minister Mrs. Indira Gandhi, and is still very popular among children.

Publisher

BUT BILLOO! DADDY IS SITTING AT THE DOOR WITH A GUN?
WHICH DOOR?
FRONT ONE!

THEN YOU CAN SLIP OUT FROM THE BACK DOOR!

TRUE! HOW USEFUL IS BACK DOOR!

I AM COMING!

WHAT? COLONEL'S DAUGHTER?

COLONEL SAHEB! IT HAS BEEN A LONG TIME, SINCE I SAW JOZI! IS SHE AT HOME?

WHY? WHERE ELSE CAN SHE GO?

LET'S BET! IF SHE EMERGES FROM HOME, I'LL PAY YOU ONE THOUSAND RUPEES, OTHERWISE, YOU PAY ME!

JOZI, DEAR!

WHAT DADDY? IF YOU CALL ME AGAIN AND AGAIN, HOW WILL I CONCENTRATE ON STUDY?
DAUGHTER! BAJARANGI WANTED TO LIGHTEN HIS POCKET!

HOW CAN THAT HAPPEN ?

HOW CAN THAT HAPPEN ?
WHY CAN'T IT HAPPEN ?

JOZI ?
BAJARANGI ! WHEN YOU SAW JOZI SLIPPING OUT — !

I KNEW YOU WOULD COMPLAIN TO HER DADDY ! I IMMEDIATELY SENT JOZI BACK HOME FROM BACK DOOR !

RAT ! I'LL GET ONE THOUSAND RUPEES FROM YOU !

GO !

WHAMM !
?!

BOW-VOW !!
HELP !

ROCK STAR

FRIENDS ! WE'RE GETTING BORED IN SUMMER VACATIONS !
THERE SHOULD BE FUN !

WE SHOULD EARN NAME !
EARN MONEY !
AND POPULARITY !
BUT HOW ?

WHY NOT MAKE A ROCK BAND ? RELEASE AN ALBUM AND GET WORLD WIDE RECOGNITION !
WOW ! SUPER IDEA !

NOW WE ARE ROCK STAR !
SHOULD WE BEGIN ?
PRAN'S FEATURES
WWW.CHACHACHAUDHARY.COM

PON !
POWN !!
ROULA-RAPPA-
ROULA-ROULA-
RAPPA-ROULA !

DO-ROULA-
RAPPA-ROULA-
RAPPA !

VACATIONS HAVE STARTED !
ROULA-RAPPA-
ADDY-TAPPA !

PON !
POWN !!
WHAT IS ALL THIS ?

STOP NOISE !

DADDY! WE'RE PRACTISING ROCK MUSIC FOR A SHOW!

WANT TO HEAR THAT!

ROULA-RAPPA-DALO-ROULA-ADDY-TAPPA ROULA-RAPPA

HOW WAS THAT?
THERE WAS NEITHER HARMONY NOR MELODY!

DAD! TIME HAS CHANGED! THIS IS ROCK MUSIC.

TRUE! A SINGER LIKE YOU WAS CALLED HARSH IN OUR TIMES. TODAY HE IS A ROCK STAR!

MAKE ALL THIS NOISE OUTSIDE ! I WANT PEACE !

IT'S DIFFICULT TO MAKE OLD GENERATION UNDERSTAND !

LET US BEGIN !

PON PON
ROULA-RAPPA-ROULA--DALO- ROULA-RAPPA !!-

WAHH ! WHAT AN IMPACTFUL VOICE ?
I BOOK YOU TO PERFORM FOR ME !

ARE YOU A MUSIC PROMOTER ?
NO !---A PROPERTY DEALER !

HOW WILL OUR MUSIC HELP IN YOUR PROFESSION ?

A STUBBORN TENANT WOULD VACATE THE HOUSE AND RUN AWAY ON HEARING YOUR ROCK MUSIC !

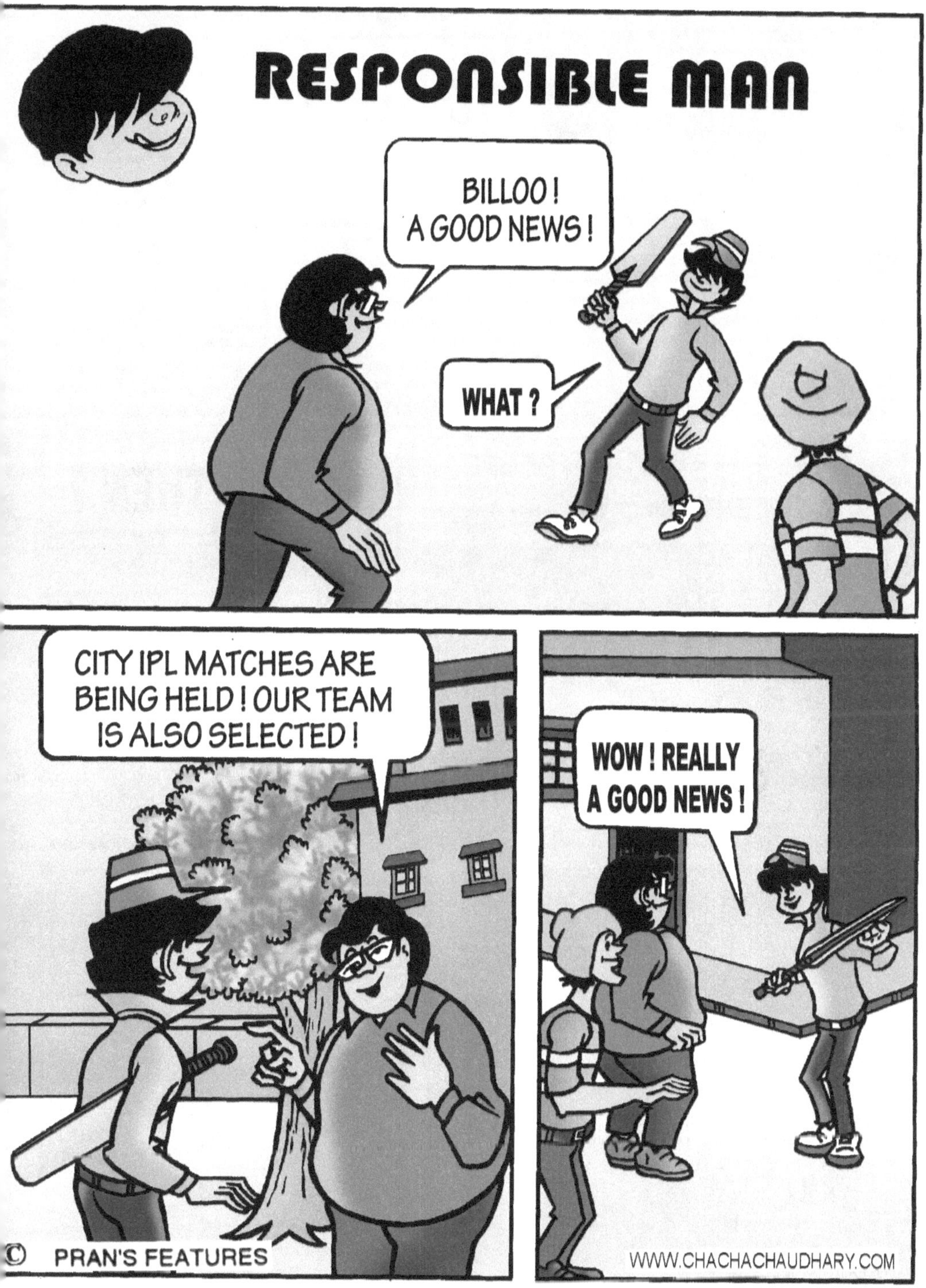

RESPONSIBLE MAN

WE WANT TO MAKE YOU OUR CAPTAIN !
BOOKS

ME ?

IS IT BECAUSE I SCORE CENTURIES ?
NO !

THEN ?

IT MAY BE BECAUSE OF MY GOOGLY BOWLING !

NO ! THERE IS SOME OTHER REASON !

IS IT BECAUSE I AM A GOOD WICKET KEEPER?
IT IS BECAUSE YOU ARE A RESPONSIBLE MAN!

THAT IS WHY WE'VE CHOSEN YOU OUR CAPTAIN!
I DID NOT UNDERSTAND!

WHENEVER A TEAM IS DEFEATED—

THEN IT IS THE CAPTAIN WHO IS BLAMED!

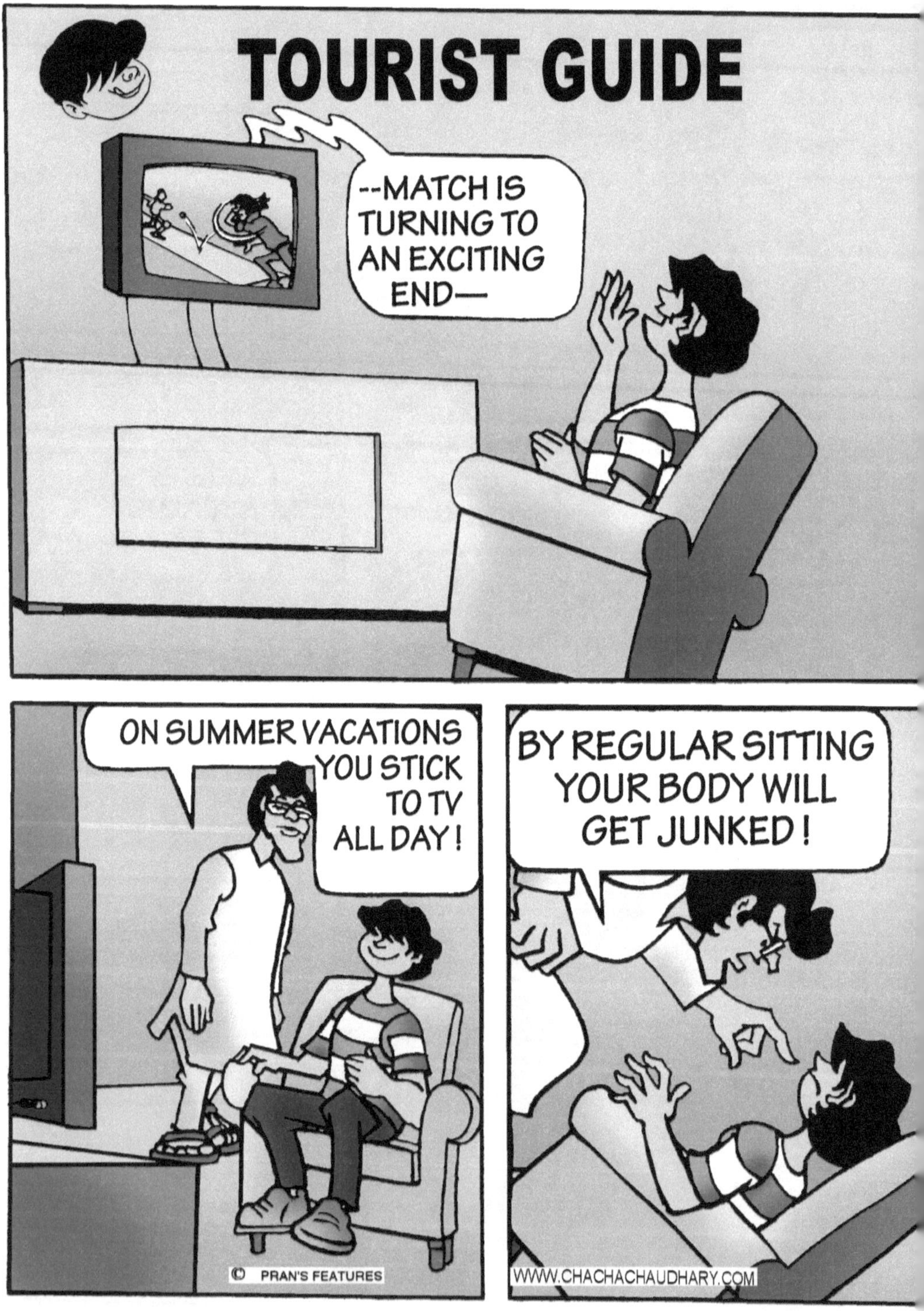

TOURIST GUIDE

DAD, WHAT JOB SHOULD I DO DURING VACATIONS ?

SUMMER TOURS OR ACTIVITIES WOULD NEED MONEY, WHICH YOU WON'T PAY ?

INSTEAD OF SPENDING, EARN !

HOW ?

FIND A SUMMER JOB !

OKAY ! GOING !
I'LLRETURN ONLY WHEN
I HAVE EARNED
MONEY !

WHO SHOULD
I CONSULT ?

GYAN CHAND ! COULD
YOU SUGGEST ANY
SUMMER JOB ?

MANY TOURISTS VISIT INDIA DURING VACATION
YOU CAN BECOME THEIR GUIDE !

THANKS
FOR THE GOOD
ADVICE !

GUIDE !---
GUIDE !!
TOURIST

COULD YOU
HELP US ?
WHY
NOT ?

FEE-TEN DOLLARS ! TAXI FARE
EXTRA !

HERE IS YOUR
MONEY !

TAXI !

SWOOSH !

THIS IS RED FORT !
CLICK!
WOW !
HOW
MAJESTIC ?

HUNDREDS
OF
LABOURERS
TOOK MANY
YEARS TO
BUILD
THAT !

LAZY INDIANS !
IN OUR COUNTRY
WE COULD CONSTRUCT
SUCH BUILDING
IN ONE YEAR !

TIME IS MONEY !

HOW MUCH TIME YOU INDIANS WASTE ?

LET US GO AHEAD !

WE HAVE A MAGNIFICENT MINARET !

LOOK, QUTAB MINAR !
WOW !
I APPRECIATE IT !

HOW MUCH TIME DID IT TAKE TO CONSTRUCT THIS?
DON'T KNOW!

THIS WAS NOT THERE YESTERDAY!

IT HAPPENS ONLY IN INDIA!

DAD! I HAVE EARNED DOLLARS!

MOTI AND LADY

BATSMAN HITS THE BALL AND RUSHES FOR RUN--!

JUMP

WHERE HAS MOTI GONE ?

LET ME CHECK ! HOPE HE IS NOT QUARRELLING !
PRAN'S FEATURES

GRRR
NO, MOTI !
WWW.CHACHACHAUDHARY.COM

GRRR

STOP !

GRRR
THE OWNER OF CAT IS VERY QUARRELSOME !

YOU STREET DOG ! YOU SCARED MY SMALL PUSSY ?
GRRR

THIS WILL CRACK YOUR HEAD !

WHAMM !

YOU ATTACKED A LADY COP ?

NO, MA'M !
I HAD HIT THE ROLLING PIN TO THE DOG !

CRUELTY ON INNOCENT ANIMALS IS EVEN A BIGGER CRIME !

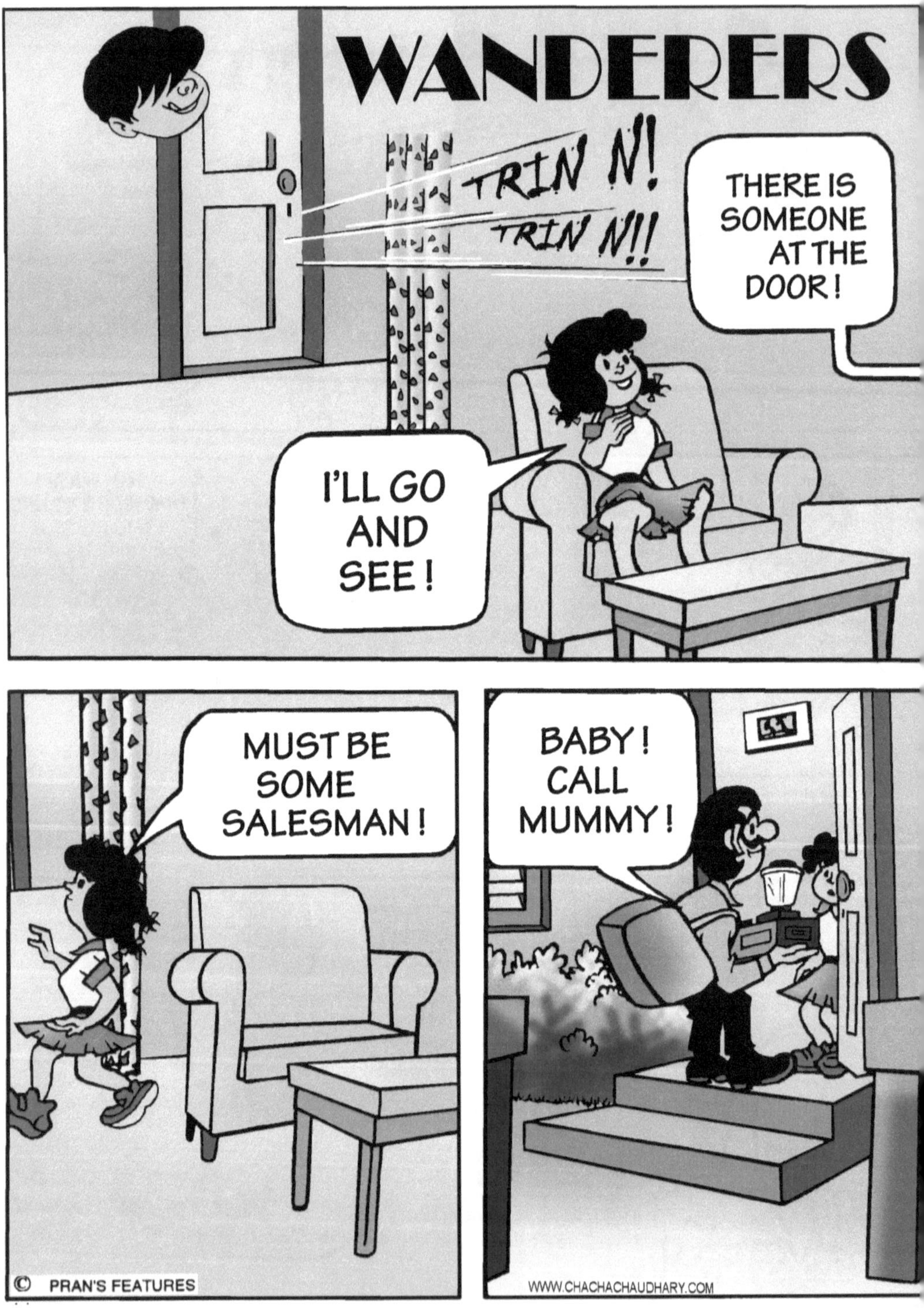

WANDERERS

24

I HAVE TO GIVE A FREE DEMONSTRATION OF MY PRODUCT!
MOM HAS GONE TO KITTY PARTY!

TODAY BEING SUNDAY, YOUR DADDY MUST BE AT HOME?
TRUE, TODAY IS DAD'S HOLIDAY!

PLEASE, CALL HIM!
HE HAS GONE TO A FRIEND'S HOUSE TO PLAY CHESS!

AND ELDER BROTHER OR SISTER?
I DON'T HAVE A BROTHER BUT MY ELDER SISTER IS THERE!

HURRY, CALL HER! SHE WOULD LIKE OUR PRODUCT!

DOES YOUR DIDI WORK IN THE KITCHEN?
YEAH!

THIS WOULD BE HELPFUL TO HER!

CALL HER! THEN I'LL START THE DEMONSTRATION!

DIDI CAN'T MEET YOU!
WHY?

SHE HAS GONE TO WATCH A MOVIE!

THE WHOLE FAMILY IS WANDERER ?

WHEN EVERYONE HAS GONE FOR AN OUTING... WHY YOU ARE AT HOME?

I HAVE COME TO MY FRIEND BILLOO'S HOUSE ! THIS IS HIS HOUSE !
?!

---AND BILLOO ALREADY HAS A MIXER ! HE WON'T BUY IT !

OH-HO !
HA ! HA !!

CAR
GLASS

WOW, MY NEW CAR!

WHAMM!

CRACK K!
??
© PRAN'S FEATURES

YOU BROKE GLASS OF MY CAR ?

YOU'LL HAVE TO PAY COMPENSATION !
HOW MUCH ?

TWO THOUSAND RUPEES !
TOO MUCH ! IF I FIX A NEW GLASS INSTEAD, HOW WOULD BE THAT ?

WHERE'LL YOU BRING A GLASS FROM ?

I WILL TAKE IT FROM MY FATHER'S CAR !
WWW.CHACHACHAUDHARY.COM

BILLOO'S
BATTING

PRACTICE MAKES A MAN PERFECT !

WAH !

THERE IS A MATCH BETWEEN ME AND MONOO IN THE EVENING !
THUMP P !
© PRAN'S FEATURES
WWW.CHACHACHAUDHARY.COM

EVENING.
BILLOO ! YOU'LL SEE HOW HARD I HIT THE BALL ?
PLEASE ! LET ME DO BATTING FIRST !

OKAY ! I'LL UPROOT THE STUMPS !

SWOOSH !!

STRIKE !

MONOO ! LOOK AT MY SIX !

HOUSE IS LOCKED !
YOU HAVE LOST MY BALL !

YOU'LL HAVE TO BUY A NEW BALL FOR ME !
SUCH THINGS HAPPEN IN A GAME !

THUMP !
THUMP !!

WHAM M!

YOU GOT YOUR BALL !--- NOW HAPPY ?

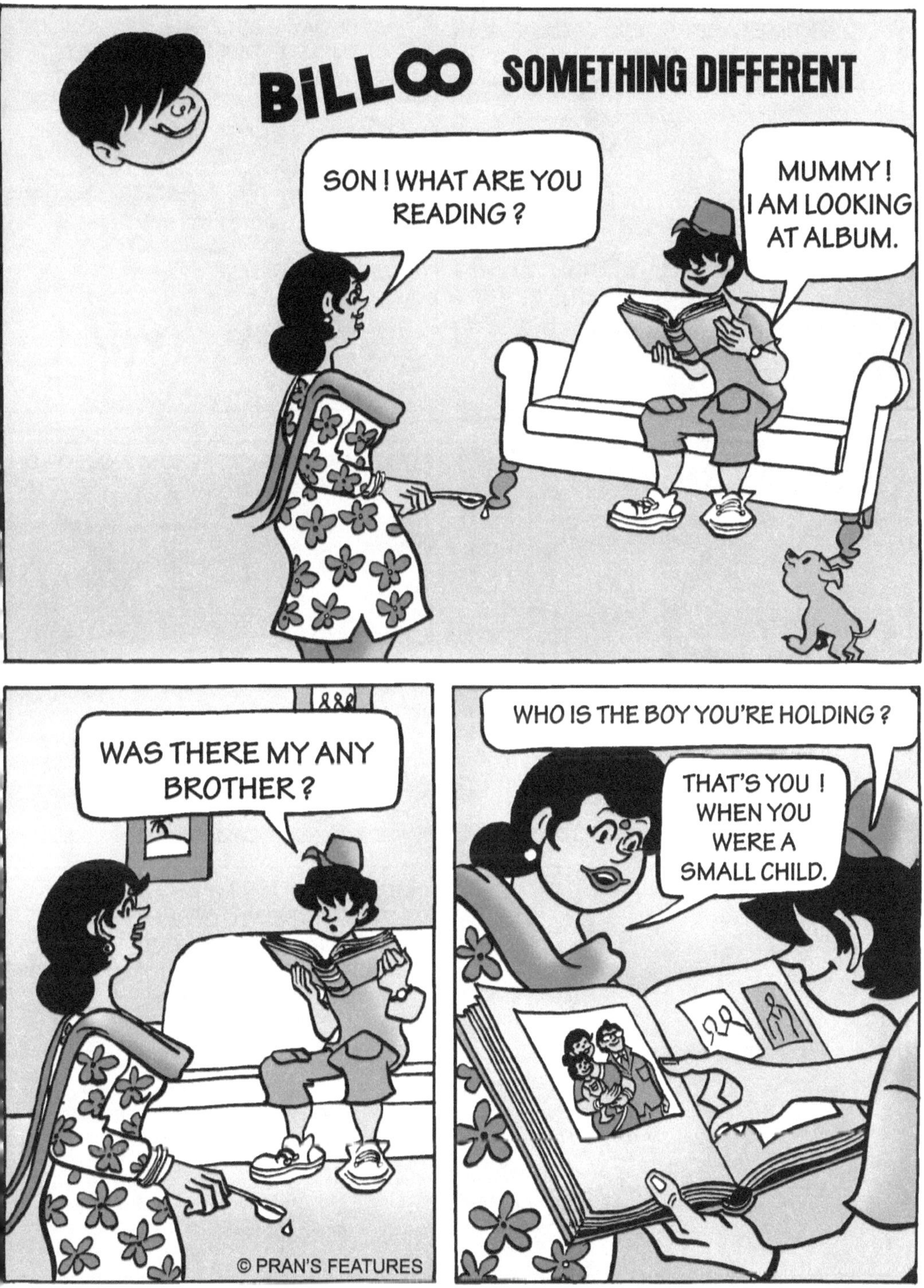

BILLOO SOMETHING DIFFERENT

AND AS TIME PASSED , YOU BECAME A TALL BOY.

AND THE DAY IS NOT FAR WHEN YOU WOULD COMPLETE YOUR EDUCATION GET EMPLOYMENT AND MARRY A SWEET GIRL !

SHOULD I ASK SOMETHING ?
GO ON !

AFTER MARRIAGE , TO WHOM WOULD YOU HANDOVER YOUR SALARY , ME OR YOUR WIFE ?

MUMMY ! AFTER MARRIAGE TO WHOM DADDY USED TO GIVE HIS SALARY , TO GRAND MOTHER OR YOU ?
www.chachachaudhary.com

YOU'VE STARTED TALKING A LOT.

WOW ! FOOD IS TASTY !

MORE CHAPATIES !
GO ON !
DON'T EAT SO MUCH WHICH MIGHT CAUSE STOMACH ACHE.

BURP ! BURP !!
YOU'RE GETTING FLATULENCE.

BURRRP !
I HAVE TO GO TO SEE JOZI - BURPP !

OH! I AM LATE! JOZI LOSES TEMPER QUITE OFTEN!

SORRY, I AM LATE!
NEVER MIND, SWEETHEART!

DEAR! I LIKE-- B-U-R-P, SITTING WITH-- B-U-R-P- YOU - B-U-R-P - AND -- B-U-R-P- CONVERSE.
BILLOO! YOU SUFFER FROM FLATULENCE.

I'LL SIT WITH YOU ONLY WHEN YOUR GAS - PASSING IS CURED.

PLEASE SIT THERE - B-U-R-P, I'LL GO - B-U-R-P HOME AND ASK - B-U-R-P - MUMMY TO TREAT – B-U-R-P – IT !

MUMMY ! GIVE SOME - B-U-R-P- HOME REMEDIES – B-U-R-P- FOR MY FLATULENCE.

TAKE AND EAT IT.
BURP.

IT IS EATEN.

JOZI ! MY GAS IS CURED.

NOW LET'S SIT AND TALK TOGETHER.

NOW YOUR MOUTH EMITS BAD SMELL OF GARLIC.

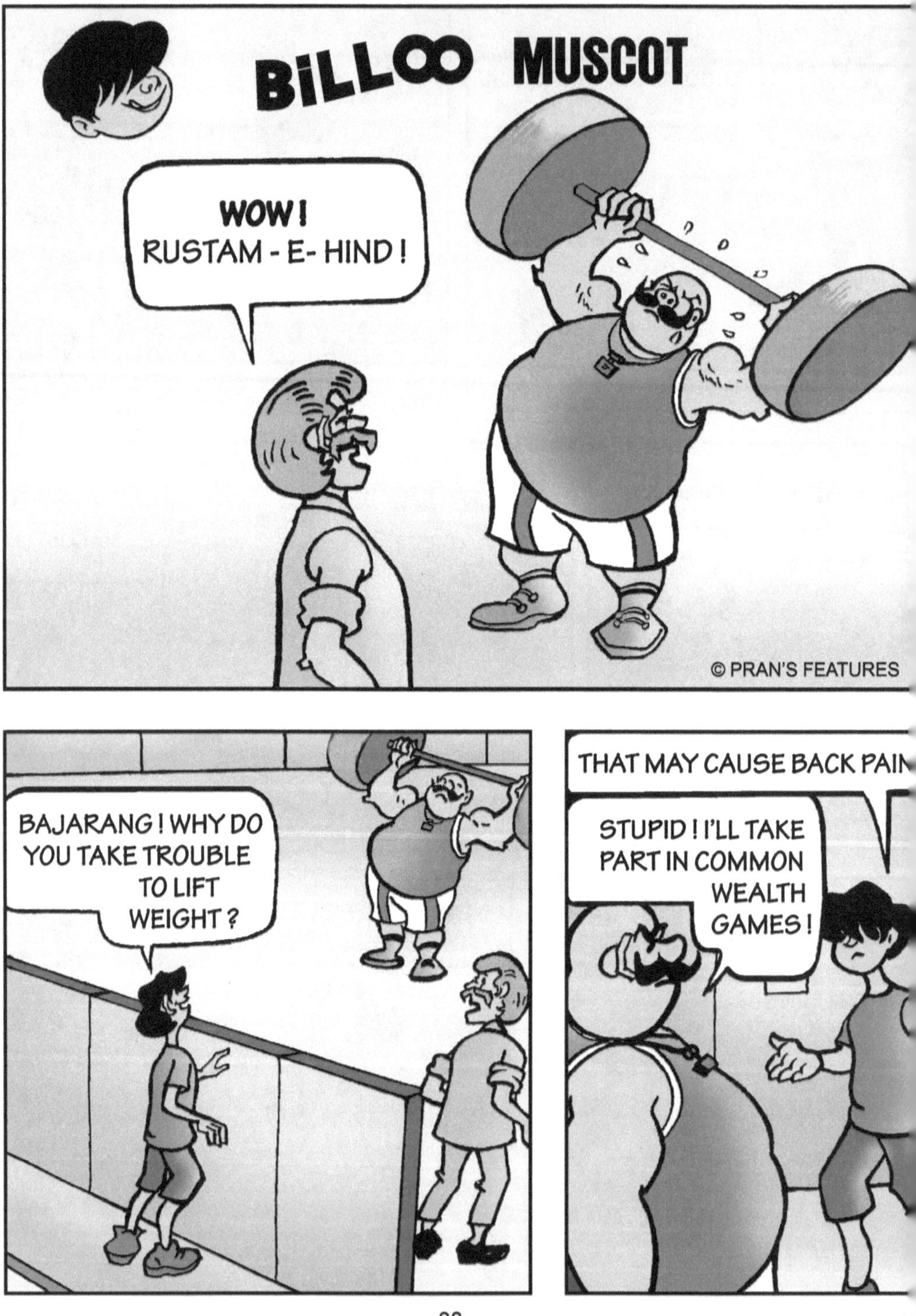

BILLOO MUSCOT

I'LL EARN GOLD MEDAL FOR MY COUNTRY.

I TOO CAN LIFT SUCH WEIGHT.
BRAGGING!

TRY AND SHOW!
OKAY!

UH-H-HI I CAN NOT EVEN MOVE IT!

GO AND WORK ON INTERNET OF COMPUTER! THIS IS NOT YOUR CUP OF TEA.

HOW ARE YOU, BILLOO ?

JOZI ! WHY ARE YOU EXERCISING ?

I'M GOING TO PARTICIPATE FOR GYMNASTICS SPORTS IN GAMES.
TOO WANT TO PARTICIPATE.

BUT IN SOME EASY EVENT.

DO YOU LIKE KARATE ?

YEAH !
THEN SHOW DEMONSTRATION

WHAMM!

OOOHH! MY FINGERS CRACKED.

BETTER YOU SIT IN STADIUM AS AN AUDIENCE!

NO! I'LL SURELY PARTICIPATE THERE.
HOW?

YOU WAIT HERE. I'LL BE BACK.
www.chachachaudhary.com

JOZI, HOW DO I LOOK ?
THAT VOICE SOUNDS SIMILAR ?
I AM BILLOO AND IT IS SPORTS GAMES MASCOT.
?!
I'LL PARTICIPATE THERE AS A MASCOT !
WOW !

© PRAN'S FEATURES

YOU HAVE RETURNED WITHOUT THE BALL. WHERE'S IT ?

SO THAT'S THE THING.

THERE THAT IS FOR YOU.

OUR BALL.
www.chachachaudhary.com

RUN THAT WAS A PLASTIC BONE. WHEN HE COMES TO KNOW THAT HE WOULD MAD AND COME AFTER US.

GRRRR !